W9-BHA-822

Other Young Yearling Books You Will Enjoy:

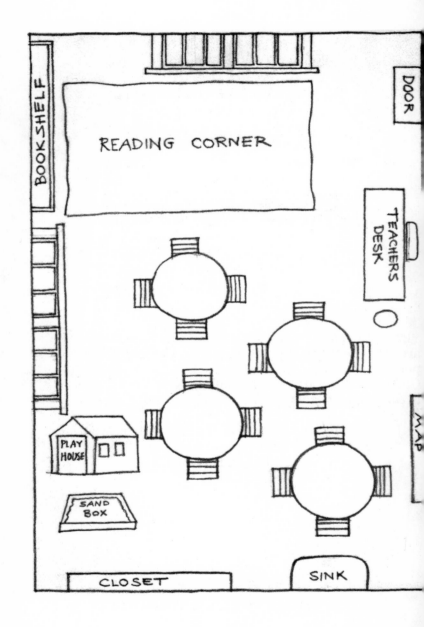

New Kids
1
at the Polk Street School

Watch Out!
Man-eating Snake

Patricia Reilly Giff

Illustrated by Blanche Sims

A YOUNG YEARLING BOOK

Published by
Dell Publishing
a division of
The Bantam Doubleday Dell Publishing Group, Inc.
666 Fifth Avenue
New York, New York 10103

ISBN: 0-440-40085-6

Printed in the United States of America

September 1988

10 9 8 7 6 5 4 3 2

W

For Sister Raymonda, C.S.J.

CHAPTER

1

Stacy Arrow opened her eyes.

Today was the day.

"School," she sang. She sang it loud. "Schooly-booly school."

She looked at the other bed.

Her sister Emily was still asleep. Her eyes were closed tight.

Stacy put her head under her sheet. "I'm afraid, fraid, fraid."

She sang it softly.

She didn't want Emily to know.

She looked across at her.

Lucky Emily.

She had the good bed.

The bouncy one.

"Wake up, old Emily," Stacy said.

Emily turned over. "It's too early. Much too early."

Stacy sat up in bed.

Her little dinky one.

She picked up Snake.

Some of his stuffing was coming out. She poked it back in.

She thought about school.

She wound Snake around her neck.

He made her feel brave.

Emily was asleep again.

"Watch out," Stacy yelled. She jumped off her bed. She landed on Emily's. "Here comes the man-eating snake."

Emily turned over. "Go back to bed."

Stacy rubbed Snake against Emily's neck.

"Poor thing," said Emily. "He has no fur left."

"He's not poor," Stacy said. "He feels nice and cool."

She put Snake under Emily's pillow.

She began to bounce.

"Kitty. Kitty. Kitty Garden," she sang. "That's me."

Emily's eyes closed.

She began to smile.

"Not kitty," she said. "You're not a cat."

Stacy took another hop. "Meow."

"Say kindergarten," Emily said.

Stacy sat down.

She touched Emily's eyelashes. Straight ones.

She tried to pull Emily's eye open. "Is kindergarten scary?"

Emily looked up at her. "Not for a big moose like you."

"A big moose with a snake," Stacy said. She tried to sound brave.

"You'll have a best friend," Emily said. "You can share things. You can tell her stuff."

Stacy gave one more bounce.

She hopped off Emily's bed.

She looked at her clothes.

Everything was ready.

Her blue top was on the chair. So was her skirt.

She looked at her shoes. Ugly blue ones.

They had holes on the top.

The holes were flowers.

Baby shoes. Baby flowers.

Her father had shined them.

She picked one up. It had two big scratches.

She pushed it under the bed.

She hid the other one in the closet.

Lucky Emily.

Emily had sneakers. New ones. They were white with purple laces.

She'd wear sneakers too.

They'd make her brave.

She'd look like a big brave moose.

A big brave moose going to cat garden.

CHAPTER
2

Stacy stood on the top step with Emily.

She moved in back of her.

She didn't want her mother to see her feet. She didn't want her to know she was wearing sneakers.

"Let me see you, Stacy," said her mother.

Stacy put her head out from behind Emily.

"Smile," her mother said. "Show your teeth. You look pretty that way."

Stacy smiled hard. She showed all her teeth. Even the back ones.

Her mother clicked the picture.

"Come on," Emily said. "We can't be late."

Emily gave her mother a quick kiss. Stacy did too.

Her mother hugged them both.

"Don't you want me to walk with you?"

"Stacy's a big girl," Emily said. "She can walk with me."

"A big moose," Stacy said.

She looked at her mother.

She wanted to say, "Come with us."

She didn't though.

"All right," her mother said.

Stacy followed Emily down the path.

She looked back.

Her mother was waving. She looked a little sad.

Stacy ran back. She gave her mother another hug. A long one.

"Stacy," Emily called. "We have to go to school."

Stacy began to run.

She really wanted to go back.

She wanted to hide in her closet.

Her mother called after her. "Where are your shoes? The ones with the flowers."

"We have to go to school," Stacy said. "We have to go right now."

They walked down the street.
They passed Mrs. Hogan's house.
Stacy swung her arms hard.

Maybe Mrs. Hogan thought she was in first grade. Maybe even second.

"First day of kindergarten?" Mrs. Hogan asked.

"Hmm," Stacy said. She pulled up her socks. They kept falling into her sneakers.

In the schoolyard everyone was running around.

Some kids were playing jump rope.

The big boys were playing ball.

Emily patted her arm. "Stand here. This is the kindergarten line."

Stacy looked down.

She couldn't see any line.

She stood there anyway.

Emily was gone.

Stacy couldn't see her anywhere.

She'd have to wait here by herself.

Maybe she was the only one in kindergarten.

She'd be all alone.

No Emily.

No kids.

Maybe no teacher.

How would she know what to do?

"Emily," she called.

Emily couldn't hear her.

Everyone was yelling. Everyone was jumping up and down.

Stacy thought about her mother. She was getting ready for work now.

She didn't know Stacy needed her.

Stacy wanted to cry.

Just then somebody came.

A mother and a little girl.

The little girl had black hair. It was straight and shiny.

Stacy smiled at her. She made sure she showed her teeth.

There's my friend, Stacy told herself. My new best friend.

The little girl didn't smile.

She didn't even look at Stacy.

She was holding on to her mother.

She was crying.

Stacy wished her mother were there too.

She wished she could hold on to her.

She wouldn't tell the girl that.

She stood up straight.

She tapped the girl on the arm.

"Stop crying," she said. "You're a big moose."

The girl looked at her.

She cried even harder.

CHAPTER
3

Now there were lots of children in line.

Mothers and fathers were there too.

The girl with the black hair was still crying.

Stacy looked at the girl's mother. "Is she a crybaby?"

The mother patted the girl's arm. "No. She's a little afraid of school."

"Really?"

"Aren't you?" asked the mother. "A little bit?"

Stacy crossed her fingers. She shook her head. "No."

A woman came over to the line.

She had books under her arm. She was jiggling keys.

Maybe she was the teacher.

Her face was round. So was her nose.

"My name is Mrs. Zachary," she said. She smiled at them. She showed all her teeth.

They were great big ones.

They stuck out a little.

Stacy smiled back at the teacher. She stuck her teeth out too.

Mrs. Zachary looked surprised. She said good-bye to the mothers. She took the children inside.

The kindergarten room was big.

It was beautiful.

Yellow and blue letters were all over the place.

The teacher's desk was in the front.

Next came tables for the children.

On one side was a sink. On the other was a sandbox and a little house.

"Pick a seat," said Mrs. Zachary.

Stacy ran to sit in the little house.

It was cozy in there. It was safe.

The girl with black hair ran too.

They got there at the same time.

They both tried to sit inside.

The girl took up all the space.

"Move over, moose," said Stacy.

She gave the girl a smile. She gave her a push too.

The girl started to cry again.

She made a lot of noise.

Some best friend she was going to be.

"Big baby," Stacy said.

Mrs. Zachary frowned. "No one

is sitting in the house right now. Sit at a table."

Stacy crawled out of the house. She went as fast as she could.

Only one table was left.

A boy was sitting there. He had big cheeks.

Next to him was a red chair. It was empty.

So was a green one.

Stacy ran for the red one.

The girl with the black hair got there first.

"I hate you," Stacy said.

She said it as low as she could.

She didn't want Mrs. Zachary to hear.

"This girl hates me," the girl told Mrs. Zachary. She put her head down on the table.

Crybaby, Stacy thought.

The teacher made round eyes at Stacy. "Sit down," she said.

Stacy sat in the green chair.

The boy smiled at her.

Stacy didn't smile back. She felt mean inside.

She had a terrible best friend.
The boy held out his fist.
She made a mean face at him.
He opened his fist.
Two raisins were in his hand.
"One for me," he said. "One for you."
Stacy changed her mean face.
She made it a smiling one.
She showed all her teeth.
"What's your name?" she asked.
"Eddie." He showed his teeth too.

"How about another raisin?" she said.

He reached into his pocket.

He took out more.

His cheeks aren't so bad, she thought.

She leaned over. She pinched one a little.

CHAPTER
4

Mrs. Zachary was standing in front of her desk.

She clapped her hands once.

Stacy sat up straight.

Emily had told her to do that.

"Now, people," said Mrs. Zachary. "We want to meet each other."

Stacy started to laugh.

No one had ever called her a people before.

Mrs. Zachary looked at her. "Try not to laugh so loud," she said.

Stacy closed her mouth.

She laughed with her lips together.

It made a nice hum-hum-hum sound.

The girl with the black hair was watching her.

She made a wrinkly face at Stacy.

Stacy stopped making the hum sound. She pointed at the girl.

Mrs. Zachary saw the girl's wrinkly face. She clicked her teeth.

Tick. Tick.

She clapped her hands again.

"This is what we'll do," she said. "Everyone will say his or her name."

"Stacy Arrow," Stacy called.

Mrs. Zachary held up her hand. "Be a good listener," she said. "Wait to hear the rest."

Stacy sat up straight.

She wanted to be a good listener.

She wanted to be the best in the class.

"We'll say our names," Mrs. Zachary said again. "We'll tell something about ourselves."

Stacy tried to think of something to tell.

She couldn't think of anything.

Not one thing.

"I'll start," the teacher said.

She sat down on the edge of her desk. "My name is Mrs. Zachary. I have a cat. His name is Tommy."

She pointed to a boy. "Your turn."

"My name is A.J.," the boy said.
His cheeks weren't fat.
They were nice and thin.
Stacy liked the look of A.J.
Too bad he didn't talk loud.
Stacy could hardly hear him.
He was telling about his dog.
Stacy wished she had a cat or a dog.
That would be nice to tell.
All she had was a hamster.
He didn't do much.

He just slept.

Sometimes he made his wheel go around.

That was no good to tell.

The girl with the shiny hair was next. She held her head up high.

"My name is Jiwon," she said.

Stacy couldn't wait to tell Emily. Her best friend was Gee One.

She wished her name were Stacy One.

"My mother came from Korea," said Jiwon. "My father did too."

"Korea is far away," Mrs. Zachary said. "It's across the ocean."

"They came on a plane," Jiwon said.

Stacy looked down at her table.

Her mother didn't come from anywhere.

Neither did her father.

Too bad.

It would be good to say they came on a plane.

It would be even better to say they came on a rocket.

Stacy laughed.

She kept her teeth closed.

She made a hum-hum sound.

Then Mrs. Zachary called on her.

Stacy stopped laughing. Everyone was looking at her. She pushed her chair back.

"My name is Stacy," she said.

She tried to think.

"At home . . ." she began.

She stopped.

She didn't say anything for a long time.

"Do you have a cat?" Mrs. Zachary asked.

She shook her head.

"How about a dog?" asked A.J.

She shook her head again.

Just then the door opened.

It was another teacher.

Mrs. Zachary went over to the door.

The children stopped looking at Stacy. They started to talk.

Stacy took a breath. "I have a snake at home."

Eddie heard her.

So did Jiwon. "You do not," she said.

"A real one?" Eddie asked.

Jiwon began to play with her hair.

She wasn't even looking at Stacy.

"He's big and scary," Stacy said.

Jiwon looked up.

Stacy took another breath. "He's a man-eater."

Mrs. Zachary came back.

"That's all about me," Stacy said.

She sat down.

She looked out the window.

CHAPTER
5

"It's time to draw," Mrs. Zachary said.

She gave out tan paper.

She gave out crayons too.

Stacy clicked her teeth.

She liked crayons with pointy tips. Not old round ones.

She picked out a red one and a blue one.

She was going to draw a boat.

A red one with a sail.

She was good at boats. Even Emily said so.

She started to make blue waves. Big sharp ones.

"We're going to draw pictures of ourselves," said Mrs. Zachary.

Stacy turned her picture over quickly. "Don't tell the teacher," she said to Eddie.

"I won't," he said. "I'm afraid of your snake."

She leaned closer.

She was going to tell him about Snake.

Jiwon was listening though.

She was making a fresh face.

"Don't worry," was all Stacy said.

"Spread out," said Mrs. Zachary. "Do a good job."

"I need to do this on the floor," Eddie said.

"Fine," said Mrs. Zachary.

"Me too," said Jiwon.

Everyone ran to the middle of the room.

They lay down on the floor.

Stacy stepped over A.J.

"Ouch," he said. "That's my foot."

"Excuse me," Stacy said in a loud voice.

She hoped Mrs. Zachary heard.

She'd think Stacy was very polite.

Stacy took a quick look at the teacher.

Mrs. Zachary was frowning a little.

Stacy showed her teeth.

Then she found a place next to Jiwon.

She started her picture.

She made a nice red head for herself.

She made pretty red lips.

She made a bunch of teeth.

Then she looked at Jiwon's paper.

Jiwon had drawn a round, fat circle.

It had loops on each side.
Everything was brown.
Poor Jiwon.
She'd help her out.
Maybe she'd tell about the snake too.

Stacy leaned closer. "Better turn your paper over. Start again."

Jiwon brushed at her bangs. "Why?"

"That's not a good job," Stacy said. "Not good at all."

"It is so." Jiwon picked up an orange crayon.

"It looks like a cow," Stacy said. "Not a girl."

Jiwon made a mean face.

"I'm just trying to help," Stacy said.

Jiwon looked at Stacy's paper. "Yours is a mess. A real mess. It looks like an apple. A silly old apple."

Stacy looked at Jiwon's paper.

She wanted to scribble on it.

She didn't though.

"How about being best friends?" she asked.

Jiwon shook her head.

"How come?"

Jiwon didn't look at Stacy.

She picked up her brown crayon.

She picked up her paper.

"I can't be friends with someone who has a snake."

Stacy opened her mouth.

"But . . ." she began.

"My mother said so." Jiwon stood up.

"Wait," Stacy said.

Jiwon didn't wait.

She went to the other side of the room.

Stacy thought for a minute.

Then she put two tears on her apple face.

CHAPTER
6

"It's time to go home," said Mrs. Zachary. "Come back tomorrow." She smiled at them. "Bring something with you. Bring something to show us."

Stacy picked up her picture.

Her mother would love it.

"Line up now," said Mrs. Zachary. "One head in back of the other."

Stacy went to the side of the room.

She put her head in back of Eddie's.

His neck was fat.

A.J. was in front of Eddie.

His neck was long and skinny.

Stacy turned around.

She wanted to see all the heads in line.

Jiwon's head wasn't right.

Her head was poking out.

Stacy wiggled one finger. "Get your head in."

Jiwon stuck out her tongue.

"Stacy." Mrs. Zachary clapped her hands.

Stacy popped her head back.

She looked at Eddie's neck again.

He had a little freckle there.

She laughed a hum-hum laugh. "Freckle Neck," she said in his ear.

Eddie banged his hand on his neck.

"I like this line," said Mrs. Zachary. "It's almost perfect."

They started down the hall.

They marched out the door.

Some children waited at the bus line.

Some ran for their mothers.

Stacy walked across the schoolyard.

Jiwon and Eddie were in front of her.

Maybe she should tell them about Snake.

Yes, she would.

"Hey," she yelled. "Wait for me."

They turned around.

Stacy put her picture under her arm. "Want to walk with me?"

Eddie looked at her.

So did Jiwon.

"Where do you live?" Jiwon asked.

"Stone Street," said Stacy. "Right down that way."

Jiwon took two steps back. "Not me. I'm not going that way."

"Me neither," said Eddie. He started to run.

Jiwon ran too. "Hurry," she yelled. "The snake may be outside."

"Yeow," screeched Eddie.

"Don't be silly," Stacy called. She tried to laugh.

She started after them.

They were way ahead of her.

"Wait," Stacy yelled. "I want to tell you something."

"Go away, snake girl," Jiwon yelled.

"Go away," called Eddie.

They didn't stop.

"I'm going to get you," Stacy said. "Me and my snake."

She stopped at the corner.

They kept going.

She sat down on the curb.

Her apple-face picture blew across the street.

She didn't care.

Kindergarten was terrible.

She wished she didn't have to go back.

CHAPTER
7

Stacy sat on the living-room floor.

She wiggled Snake around the table.

She thought about Jiwon.

She wanted to cry.

"Move over a little," Emily said. "I have to wrap this."

Stacy looked up.

"It's Jill Simon's birthday," said Emily. "I'm going to her party."

Stacy stuck her lip out.

She'd never go to Jiwon's party. Never.

"What's the matter?" Emily asked.

Stacy raised one shoulder.

"Did you find a friend in school?"

"Snake is my friend." Stacy shook him back and forth.

"Boring friend." Emily spread out the wrapping paper.

Emily was right, Stacy thought. "I did find a friend," she said.

"Good."

"No good," said Stacy. "She doesn't like me."

Emily put a box on the paper. "Why not?"

"I don't know." Stacy crossed her fingers.

She put Snake under the couch.

Emily looked at her. "You have to be nice to a friend."

"I'm nice," Stacy said. "Everybody thinks so."

"You have to be kind," Emily said.

"I'm kind," said Stacy. "Kinder than anybody."

Emily put tape on the paper. "You have to do things for a friend."

"I did," said Stacy. "I told her to do her picture over."

"Maybe you hurt her feelings," said Emily.

"Maybe she's a big baby," Stacy said.

Emily took Stacy's finger. "Hold

it here. On the ribbon. I want to make a bow."

"It looks nice, Emily," said Stacy. "Very nice."

Emily sighed. "It's hard to make bows. It looks like a mess."

"My friend is a mess too," said Stacy.

"Really?" said Emily.

"Yes. She took up all the room in the playhouse. She told the teacher I hate her."

Stacy made a face. "She even has the best chair. A red one."

"What color is your chair?" Emily asked.

"No-good green," Stacy said.

Emily laughed a little.

Stacy made eyes like Mrs. Zachary's. Big round ones. "That's not funny."

Emily picked up the paper.

She picked up the ribbon.

She put them in the kitchen.

Stacy sat there.

She wished she were getting a present.

Jill was lucky.

Emily was a good friend.

She closed her eyes.

Then she thought of something.

"Hey, Emily," she called. "I need the rest of the paper."

"All right."

"The ribbon too?" Stacy asked.

"I guess so."

Stacy stood up.

She had a wonderful idea.

She hoped it would work.

CHAPTER
8

Stacy poured chocolate milk into her Sugar Puffs.

"Yuck," said her mother.

"Two times yuck," said her father.

"Hurry," said Emily. "I want to be early."

Stacy ate her cereal fast.

It was great.

She drank her juice slowly.
It wasn't so great.
She hated grapefruit juice.
It made her cheeks stick together.
Besides, she didn't want to hurry.
She was worried about her idea.
Maybe it wasn't so good.
Maybe Jiwon wouldn't like it.
Emily was waiting.

"I have to get something," Stacy told her.

"Get your pretty shoes," said her mother. "Those sneakers are terrible."

Stacy shook her head.

Her hair flew in her face.

"Stacy," her mother said. "I mean it."

Stacy made Mrs. Zachary eyes.

She went upstairs.

She put on her no-good shoes with the holes.

She grabbed her present.

She raced downstairs.

"What's that?" Emily said.

Stacy looked at it.

The paper was a little wrinkled.

So was the bow.

It had tons of tape on it.

"It's a surprise," said Stacy. "Does it look all right?"

"Gorgeous," said Emily.

"I thought so," said Stacy.

They went down the street.

They went into the schoolyard.

"See you later," said Emily.

Stacy looked around.

Jiwon was sitting on the sandbox.

Stacy skipped over to it.

She was a great skipper.

She was glad Jiwon was looking at her.

Jiwon didn't say anything though.

Neither did Stacy.

They just sat there for a while.

Then Jiwon looked up.

"Whose birthday?"

"Yours," said Stacy.

"It is not," said Jiwon. "Mine was last month."

"It's for you anyway," said Stacy.

Jiwon held her hands out. "All right."

"Lots of tape on it," said Stacy.

Jiwon nodded. "Hard to get open."

"I hope you like it," Stacy said. "It's a little old."

Jiwon pulled off a piece of the paper.

She could see one orange eye.

"It's a man-eater," said Stacy.

Jiwon tore off the rest of the paper. "That's the snake?"

"Yep," said Stacy. "There he is."

"Whew," said Jiwon.

"Yep," said Stacy again.

The bell rang.

Jiwon put the snake around her neck.

They both stood up.

"Hey," said Stacy. "You have no-good shoes."

"Just like yours." Jiwon held up one foot. "Watch out," she yelled to Eddie. "I've got the man-eater."

"Watch out," Stacy called too.

She grabbed Jiwon's hand.

They ran for the line.